PUFFIN BOOKS

HIGH WATER
AT CATFISH BEND

It is the year of the most terrible flood in the history of the Mississippi, and five animals have climbed onto a small flood mound built by neighboring farmers to save their horses and cattle. The animals are Doc Raccoon, later the Mayor of Catfish Bend; Judge Black, the motto-quoting black snake who has become a vegetarian to clear the snake family's bad name; J.C., the sporty, fast-talking red-haired fox from Memphis; the silly rabbit; and the gloomy frog, whose only joy is directing the Indian Bayou Frog Glee Club. The black snake, when his lower nature grips him, is tempted to eat the frog; the fox is hungry for the rabbit. Unlike most warring humanity, they suddenly realize that if they are to survive, they must unite against the common enemy, the flood. With the high water over at last, they set out for New Orleans to demand that the riverbanks be made safe for wild animals. The strange and perilous adventures that befall them reveal that animals have much the same problems these days as human beings.

BEN LUCIEN BURMAN

HIGH
WATER AT
CATFISH BEND

Illustrations by ALICE CADDY

Puffin Books

Penguin Books Ltd, Harmondsworth, Middlesex, England
Penguin Books, 625 Madison Avenue, New York, New York 10022, U.S.A.
Penguin Books Australia Ltd, Ringwood, Victoria, Australia
Penguin Books Canada Limited, 2801 John Street, Markham, Ontario,
    Canada L3R 1B4
Penguin Books (N.Z.) Ltd, 182–190 Wairau Road, Auckland 10,
    New Zealand

First published by Taplinger Publishing Company, Inc., 1952
Published in Great Britain by Kestrel Books 1975
Published in Puffin Books 1974
Reprinted 1977

Library of Congress Cataloging in Publication Data
Burman, Ben Lucien.   High water at Catfish Bend.
    Summary: Caught in a Mississippi flood, a group of
animals takes over the problem of flood control from the
incompetent humans.
    [1. Animals—Fiction. 2. Floods—Fiction]
I. Caddy, Alice. II. Title.
PZ7.B9268Hj 1977   [Fic]   77-13925
ISBN 0 14 03. 0711 7

Printed in the United States of America
by Offset Paperback Mfrs., Inc., Dallas, Pennsylvania
Set in Janson

It was lucky for me that the *Tennessee Belle* stopped along the Mississippi to pick up some cotton just where she did that afternoon. If she hadn't stopped, I never would have heard the truth about those queer things that went on in New Orleans. But I'd better put it down, just the way it happened.

We were waiting at Catfish Bend, just below Vicksburg, and I was watching the towboats go past loaded with lumber and automobiles, when I saw an old raccoon come out of a hollow tree behind me and sit down on the bank. A minute later a young raccoon trotted up and sat down by him, and they began eating some red berries growing on a bush. And they began talking about the steamboats, the way everybody does that lives on the river—which one could go fastest, and which one had the prettiest whistle.

After a while a workboat of the Government Engineers chugged up the river, and stopped on the other shore where some men were building one of those big earth walls they call a levee,

to keep the river from flooding and washing away everybody's houses. The two raccoons began talking about that, and I wasn't paying much attention. And all of a sudden the old one said something that made me prick up my ears. Then I listened hard. But you know the way it is when you want to hear something special, the people always stop talking. In a few minutes they finished the berries and the young coon went away.

The old coon sat there by himself, poking at an anthill with his paw. He looked friendly, ready for company, so after a while I went over and we started talking. He had a nice face, and honest, too. You knew right off you could believe what he told you. I didn't ask him

what I wanted at first. Animals are very touchy sometimes, and I didn't like to take chances on scaring him away.

A paper bag in my coat pocket rattled and his eyes began to shine. "You wouldn't happen to have a chocolate bar handy, would you?" he asked.

I always have plenty of chocolate bars when I ride on steamboats. I gave him a big one, with a lot of nuts inside.

He rolled the silver wrapper into a ball and put it down a hole in the tree.

"I'm saving the papers," he said.

He picked out a nut and chewed it for a minute. His fur was pretty ragged, as if he'd knocked about quite a bit, and the end of his tail was missing, as if he'd been caught in a trap.

"What's your name?" he asked.

I told him.

"Mine's Doc," he said. "Glad to know you. I've seen you fooling around here on the shantyboats and steamboats. I'm kind of a tramp myself."

I put out my hand. He shook it, and then washed his paw for almost a minute in the river. "No offense," he said. "It's just the way we raccoons have of doing. So many germs everywhere."

The Engineer boat began scooping earth from the river and piling it up on the opposite shore to make the levee higher.

"Looks like they're really stopping the floods around Catfish," I said.

"About time," the raccoon answered, sort of mumbling because his mouth was stuffed full of candy.

"You were telling something to that young raccoon a while ago," I said, hoping to get him started.

He wiped some chocolate off his whiskers. "Oh that," he answered.

He polished the whiskers until each hair was shiny as wax. "I was telling him how most people think it was the farmers around here that got together, and made the Government fix up these levees and things so the river wouldn't cover up everything in high water. But

I can tell you it wasn't. Like to hear the real story?"

"I've been trying to find out a long time," I told him.

"Well, credit where credit's due," he answered. "The truth never hurt anybody."

He looked out over the river, thinking. "It wasn't the farmers around here that stopped the floods at all. It was the animals."

And this is the story he told me. I've had to switch a name or two, the way he asked. He didn't want to get any animals in trouble. Otherwise I haven't changed a word.

The raccoon began:

I

WE'VE always had terrible floods here at Catfish. Well, this one I'm going to tell you about was the worst ever. The land was covered over as far as you could see, and there wasn't a house showing anywhere. Nothing but muddy water, racing and boiling. Only one tree was left, that'd been the tallest tree around here, and so much of it was under the river the part that was showing didn't look much bigger than a blackberry bush. I was up in the top branches, watching the water come higher and higher, and wondering how much longer I'd be alive. I stayed in the tree a couple of days, I guess, and then one morning, just after the sun was up, I saw a terrible wave coming down the river, so big and black it looked like a tornado, only this was water instead of being up in the sky. And in a minute I was all swallowed up, and everything went dark as the inside of a possum's stomach, and I thought it was the finish.

Pretty soon, though, things began to get light again, and I saw the big wave had passed. But my tree was gone, and

I was out in the middle of the flood.

I swam for hours, I guess. Every once in a while I'd get all choked up with water from some big wave, and I'd think I was going to drown, and then I'd manage to go on again. But you can't last forever. And I was beginning to get weak and dizzy, and everything was spinning round and round like the whirlpools in the water. And I knew I couldn't keep my head up much longer.

And then I saw one of those mounds of earth people here build for their cows and horses to climb on when the floods come so they won't drown. This mound was a quarter of a mile away, and my strength was almost gone. But I managed to get close to it, and caught hold of a branch and pulled myself ashore.

And then everything went black again.

When I came to I was lying on the bank, and a big old bullfrog was sitting there, watching me with his bulgy eyes.

He was a gloomy old fellow, with his skin hanging down in wrinkles, reminded you of one of those turkey buzzards that go around all the time looking for animals to bury. You could see he'd had a lot of trouble in his life.

"You'd be better off dead," he croaked. "It's the only land in a hundred miles. It's the end of the world."

His voice was so deep it was like the bottom note of a steamboat calliope.

I didn't have the strength to answer. I just lay there, panting for breath.

"Anybody else here?" I asked, when I was able to breathe a little better.

"There's a kind of a rabbit," he croaked.

The rabbit came over in a few minutes, rubbing his eyes, for he'd been taking a nap. He spoke to me, and looked at the water. "Carrots!" he said. "It's getting higher and higher."

He stayed there, talking. I was feeling stronger now, and sat up and looked him over. And what I saw didn't make me too happy. When you've just saved yourself from drowning, and you don't know what's going to happen next, you like to have somebody around that you can depend on. He was a nice enough rabbit, I guess. But he was sort of silly, talking in a high, squeaky voice, and giggling all the time like a girl. And his tail was never still a minute. A tail's the real way to tell a person's character; a tail's something you ought to use with care. I'm not so crazy about cats. They give me plenty of worry when I tangle up with 'em around a farmhouse at night. But I will say they know how to handle a tail, slow, thoughtful. You can see with every swing how much brain there is behind it. The rabbit's tail was going like a hummingbird's wing all the time. You knew right away he didn't have a grain of sense in his head. And you knew he wouldn't be any help when you got into real trouble.

All morning we sat at the edge of the mound, watching the river keep on rising. And every once in a while we'd have to move back a little, because the water had come up to the place where we'd been sitting. And the mound kept getting smaller and smaller.

"It's the end of the world," croaked the frog again, wiping off some mud from the wrinkles in his face. "Just when I was beginning to enjoy things a little, too. They started a new frog Glee Club at Indian Bayou, and they made me leader. I had 'em tuned just right. And you don't know how hard it is to tune a frog. Now the Club's scattered all over the Mississippi. I guess we'll never sing again."

All of a sudden he stopped talking, and gave a jump that sent him all the way across the mound. And a second later the rabbit went jumping right behind.

And then I saw the reason. A big black snake—maybe five feet long—was coming down the river, so worn out every wave would knock him under,

almost the way it was with me a few hours before. I don't like snakes better than anybody else, but of course black snakes aren't like moccasins or rattlers, they're really all right. And I hate to see anything in trouble. So I held out a long branch, and he caught it, and I pulled him toward the shore.

"Black's my name," he panted, when he landed. "Judge Black. From Grand Gulf in Claiborne County, Mississippi. I'll never forget you."

He coiled up on a log for a while, and then he saw the frog and the rabbit, shivering on the other side of the mound, trying to look like the grass.

He got very worried. "Tell them not to be afraid," he said. He hissed a little when he spoke. But it was a soft hiss and didn't bother you.

I called the others over, but they wouldn't move.

The snake was very sad. "It's terrible to have a bad reputation. But I'm doing everything I can to live it down. I'm a vegetarian. Never eat meat and never bother anybody. Only when my lower nature starts to get the better of me. And then you can see in plenty of time. My eyes get fuzzy around the edges."

I told the frog and the rabbit, and after a while they came over, though you could see they were pretty nervous. They were all talking and seemed to be getting along fine, when the black snake shivered.

He stared at the frog and the rabbit for a minute, and then all of a sudden he turned his head away. "You'd better go off to the other end of the mound," he said. "I'm terribly tired and hungry. And I think my eyes are getting on the fuzzy side."

They bolted off so fast you could almost hear the air whistle, and they didn't come back for a couple of hours.

Lunchtime came, and suppertime, and there wasn't anything to eat or to look at even, only the water and the mound getting narrower all the time. And every once in a while there'd be a terrible bump and the mound would shake like it was going to sink into the river, and then we'd see it was a big tree that hit the edge, and washed away again.

The sun set, and it started to get dark.

A log came racing down the current, and in the twilight I saw a shadow sitting on it, steering with a piece of board. At first I thought the shadow was a boy, but when it came closer I saw it was a fox. He guided the log to the mound, and when it touched, jumped off in a hurry.

He was one of those sporty foxes, red-haired, and red-faced, and talked fast and loud. He looked like some of those smart-aleck fellows that come down to the swamps from Memphis and those other places to fish on Sundays, with their hair slicked back and wearing fancy clothes.

"Always room for one more, ain't

that right, folks?" he said. "It's your friend J. Hunter, folks. J. C. Hunter. Just call me Jaysee."

He saw the rabbit and gave me a big wink. "A Triple A," he chuckled. And when I asked him what he meant he leaned over to whisper in my ear. "It's rabbit golf," he said. "That's what we foxes call it when we chase 'em. An old brown rabbit counts one, a young brown rabbit two, and a young cottontail like that's Triple A—that's the best of all. I've had the rabbit-catching championship at Catfish two years in a row."

The rabbit heard, and even though it was getting dark, I could see his whole body turn almost as white as his tail.

The fox winked again. "Would have

won the championship of the state last year, but I lost the rabbit's foot I always carried for luck," he said.

The rabbit gave a terrible gulp and choked on something he'd been eating, looked like a turnip top. His face got redder and redder and it seemed as if he was going to choke to death. But I grabbed one hind leg and the snake took the other, and we held him upside down. And pretty soon the turnip top fell out, and he could breathe again. But he lay on the ground without moving a long time.

I was pretty angry at the fox. "Please watch your language," I said to him. "After all, you're a guest here."

He said he would, but I could tell from his eyes he didn't mean it.

Judge Black looked at him a long time. "Honorable is as honorable does," he said, because being a judge he knew a lot of mottoes.

He cleared his throat and put a little pill in his mouth. "My own kind of cough drops," he explained. "Made of beeswax and slippery elm. I have to talk all the time on the bench and I always watch my throat. A snake's throat's so long, you know. When it does get sore there's so much to hurt."

Well, it got late, and everybody was worn out and lay down on the grass to try to get some rest. But nobody slept really. The frog was watching the snake, and the snake was watching the rabbit, and the poor silly rabbit was watching the fox, and I was watching

all of them. A couple of times I saw the fox's mouth watering, and he'd pretend to be sleeping, and then give a big roll that brought him close to the rabbit. And I'd wait till he got a couple of raccoon tails away, and then I'd call out, and he'd get up and look mad, and then he'd start all over.

Once the frog woke and gave a terrible cry. I rushed over to him, wondering what happened.

"Had a nightmare," he said, shivering the way only a frog can shiver. "I thought I saw a snake."

Then he saw the snake really there beside him, and he remembered. "It's the end of the world," he croaked.

And Judge Black just shook his head and looked sad.

II

ALL NIGHT long it was that way, one thing after another, just trouble and worry for everybody. And a few feet away the water kept rushing past, tearing at the mound so hard you didn't know whether it would last till morning. And you heard queer sounds all the time, sad sounds, steamboats out looking for drowning people or trying to get into a harbor, or animals going down on driftwood, calling out for help that nobody could give them, or birds flying overhead and chirping, looking for their nests and their babies they'd never see again.

Morning came, and everybody got

up more tired than when they lay down, because nobody slept a wink. We looked at the mound and saw that it was half the size it'd been the day before. The river had come up a couple of feet in the night. And I saw we'd have to do something.

I was the oldest raccoon around

Catfish, and sort of used to running things, so I called all the animals together. I smoothed down my fur, because I know I look a little rumpled sometimes. "We can't go on like this," I said. "We can't tell what'll happen. Maybe the river's going to keep on getting higher, and we'll have to be busy every minute to stop the mound from being washed off. Or if we don't all get drowned, we'll have to be here for weeks, anyway. I've seen this high water last two months sometimes. If we stay there's going to be plenty of work for everybody, keeping the mound in shape, and trying to find enough to eat to keep alive. We can't go on just watching each other day and night every minute. We'd all go crazy."

Judge Black cleared his throat and took a cough drop. I could see he was as worried as I was. "What do you think we ought to do?" he asked.

I slicked back my whiskers and looked as important as I could. "We've got to sign a pact," I said.

"What's a pact?" asked the rabbit, who I told you didn't know very much.

"A pact's blood brotherhood," I answered. "The animals should have made a pact when they came out of the Ark after Noah's Flood, but they didn't. Think of all the hurt paws and scratched hides and scarred faces they'd have saved themselves by not fighting in all that time. We've been pretty near as bad as people."

A murmur went up from the other

animals. Even the fox looked hurt. "It'd be terrible if animals were as bad as people," he said.

"Well, this time there won't be any mistakes," I told them. "We'll all take an oath never to claw or bite, and work

together paw in paw, and stand by each
other no matter what the danger."

"United we stand. Divided we fall,"
said Judge Black, with his mottoes again.

I expected an argument, but there
wasn't any. Everybody saw it was the

only thing to do. Even the fox looked as if he meant what he said. You feel pretty helpless and lonesome when you're on a tiny little mound surrounded by hundreds of miles of flood water that's eating away the earth you're standing on by inches. It's too bad everybody in the world can't be on a little island the same way. Maybe they'd learn how to get along better. Anyway we all swore the oath and became blood brothers.

"What about it when we feel ourselves slipping back a little?" asked the Judge. "I haven't had any breakfast yet, and my eyes get a little fuzzy when I look at the frog."

"Somebody'll say Ararat," I answered. "That's the code word. Then everybody'll think of the Ark and how foolish the animals were not to make friends back in the old times."

"When I get to thinking about rabbits my tail starts thumping," declared the fox. "Then somebody better say Ararat fast."

The water rose a little more in the morning. But it didn't wash away the mound. And we piled some driftwood and logs around the edges to help as much as we could. We were getting mighty hungry, but lucky for us a couple of loaves of bread and some oranges came floating down from somebody's kitchen that'd been flooded, and I swam out with the frog and caught them and we had a pretty good meal. Around sunset we could see that the water wasn't coming up any more, and we all felt better.

Well, we were on the mound pretty near six weeks, the way I remember. We all did the things we knew the best. I did all the washing, because that's a raccoon's specialty, and the frog would always fetch the things in the river, because he was the best swimmer. The fox used to sweep up the place every morning, because his tail made the best  broom, and the snake did all the polishing up, his skin was so slippery. The rabbit didn't have sense enough to do anything by himself, so he just helped everybody. That is he'd start to help, and then first thing you knew, he was off nibbling a plant or chasing a puff-ball blowing along the ground.

But the rest of us kept the place as nice and clean as a beaver picnic grounds. If a big log that was covered with oil and was all smelly would float in, we'd get together and push it away. And we took turns keeping watch, day and night. It wasn't easy, I can tell you. Sometimes we almost went crazy, just waiting and waiting for the water to fall. But we managed to stay alive.

A good many times the snake's eyes started getting fuzzy, and the fox's tail began pounding the earth like a drum. And then somebody'd call out "Ararat," and everything'd be all right again.

Then one day we saw a whole family of chipmunks floating down on a log from a new washout somewhere. And I said it looked terrible to me that every year we had to go through these floods, with thousands and thousands of animals getting killed, and those that weren't killed being driven out of their homes they'd been to so much trouble building, and taking their children somewhere else and having to start all over.

"Maybe when the flood's ended we ought to talk to the animals live on the farms around here," I said. "Maybe we can fix up some way to get the farmers to go down to New Orleans and see the Engineers and ask them to build some levees and spillways and things, so we don't have high water any more. They've got the floods fixed fine at New

Orleans, and they can fix 'em for us, too. Animals can make people do plenty of things, without their knowing about it. We've got the pact now. If we wild animals and farm animals at Catfish all stick together, there isn't anything we can't do."

"Do or die," said Judge Black.

There wasn't much argument about that either.

Well, the river finally went down, and we all raced around in every direction, even if it was sticky with mud, we were so tired of being cooped up on the mound. And for a few days we forgot what we'd been through. And then the water started coming up again, the way it does so often. And we knew we'd have to get busy.

I went over to see an old horse I knew, lived on a place owned by the smartest farmer around here. It wasn't much of a farm to look at, because the floods were always washing things away, and the horse wasn't so wonderful looking, either, a kind of grouchy old fellow, with his back caved in and his mouth always so full of hay you could hardly understand what he was saying. But I'd known him for a long time, and we got along all right.

I found him outside the stable munching some corn in a trough, and I gossiped with him for a while about the man he worked for that I could see fixing a fence, a big man, always wore overalls and a big straw hat. He was a fine fellow, always left nice things in his garbage cans at night for an animal to eat, and wouldn't put the lid on too tight, so you could get it loose without waking all the dogs and having to run for your life. Most of the people at Catfish were like that, too, and we woods animals tried to show we appreciated it. We never scattered their garbage once. There are two kinds of people, tight-lid people and loose-lid people. There are some tight-lid people I could tell you about, where I've seen an animal take

just a few mouthfuls of garbage and scatter it over a
mile.

I told the horse what
we'd been talking about, and
how we thought the people
around there ought to go down to New
Orleans.

He looked at me in his grouchy kind
of way, and stripped a cob of corn clean
before he answered. "You woods animals don't know much, do you?" he
grumbled. "If you'd kept your eyes and
ears open you'd know what's been happening. The farmers here have made a
hundred trips to New Orleans, I guess.
I've taken my farmer ten times myself,
anyway. The floods around here keep
everybody too poor to have auto-

mobiles. Well, each trip the farmers go to the Government Engineers, and the Engineers say they've got no time for 'em. They say they have to put up a hurricane wall near Gulfport, and they've got to deepen the channel where the ocean ships run to Houston, and maybe they've got to put up a new Panama Canal, since the one down there's getting so crowded. And then the farmers go to see the Mayor. He's the big bale of hay in New Orleans. If they can get him to say he'll do something, they're all right with the Engineers or anybody. So they ask him to help. But he tells 'em no, the same way. The New Orleans people have got their levees and cutoffs so they're all safe now, and they've forgotten the way it used to be. They're not going to worry about this country up river where there's just a few poor swamp fellows raising boll weevils and hogs. I heard my farmer talking yesterday. He and some of the rest of them are going down in a few weeks again to see what they can do. But I know what'll happen. They'll just be wasting time."

I went back and told the others what happened. And while we were talking I had an idea. "Looks to me like we ought to go down to New Orleans and see what we can do ourselves," I said.

We talked it over, and we all were willing except the rabbit. He was always afraid of everything.

"We'll never get there," he said. "There's millions of moccasins and

that worried us a little, because spiders, like rats, know when there's going to be trouble.

Well, we patched up all the cracks with moss and dirt, and then the frog came on with the Indian Bayou Glee Club, about thirty of them, I guess, tiny lady frogs with voices like crickets, and

big bullfrogs that when they sang together sounded like logs bumping down a mountain. Funny thing about the frog. When he was by himself he was always kind of quiet and gloomy, but now when all the little frogs were around he got bossy, and was always telling them what to do. And his stomach would swell up in little jerks, till it looked like a watermelon breathing.

We counted the passengers to see that we hadn't left anybody behind, then let the lines go and started down the river. Everywhere along the shore the water was coming up through the willows, and we knew that Catfish was in for a bad flood again.

Except for that everything looked wonderful. The sun was shining, and the big white cranes flew back and forth in front of us asking us all the time what was going on, and everybody was glad they'd come.

All of a sudden when we were out in the middle of the river, we saw a cloud moving over the water. It wasn't a big cloud at first, but quicker than you can say it, the sky was gone, and you couldn't see anything except rain and lightning. The waves threw us up and they threw us down, and the shanty-boat began to leak all over. And there was an awful crash, and I knew we'd hit something. Then the lightning flashed, and I saw the water pouring through a big crack in the bottom. It looked for a minute as if we might as well have died on the mound, because

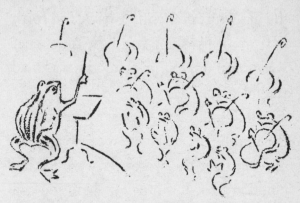

we were going to die here mighty fast, the way the water was getting deeper and deeper. But we managed to get the leak plugged up, and we all started bailing. And pretty soon the rain and the lightning stopped, and the sun came out, and the storm was over.

And the frog got the Indian Bayou Glee Club together, and showed us how they could imitate a steamboat calliope, and everybody had a fine time.

It was nice watching the country go by. We went past a placed called Frogmore, and the frog all puffed up and looked terribly proud. And then the rabbit got all excited when we saw a place called Rabbit Hill. But a little while later we came to a place called Rabbit Hash, and the poor rabbit turned white as cotton, and went inside the shantyboat and didn't come out again till dark.

The second day started out nice and bright like the first, and then it got all dark again, only this time not from a storm but from a fog, the worst fog I ever saw. You couldn't see a paw before your face, even if it was touching your whiskers. I didn't know what we were going to do. There were big towboats

everywhere that would break us into pieces, and all kinds of docks and barges along the shore that we'd smash into if we didn't keep to the channel, and sand bars we'd be stuck on for the rest of our lives, and never get to New Orleans.

And then the frog hopped up to me with his stomach going in jerks, the way it did whenever he felt important. "I'll get you through," he croaked.

I asked him how, for I couldn't see anything but the fog, and it was getting thicker and thicker.

"A frog's the best fog pilot there is

anywhere," he croaked again. "Frogs aren't like people or cats. Each of 'em sings just one note. And all my frogs sing different. One sings *do* and one sings *re*, another sings *mi* and another *fa*. We'll let all the frogs swim ahead of the boat and go out to the bank or wherever there's a barge or anything solid, and mark both sides of the channel. Then we can start down and call to 'em. And they can call back, and we'll know where we are, as long as we can hear the voices."

We anchored the boat right away, and the frogs swam out to their places. And then the big frog stood beside me, and we started down the water. Every once in a while he'd give a loud croak, and a note would come out of the blackness in answer. "That's *fa*," he would say. "Swing a little to the left." He'd call again, and this time a deeper note would come. "That's *do*," he'd croak. "Pull her hard to the right."

We kept this up all morning, passing steamboats and Government boats and every kind of boat you could think of, looking like ghosts in the mist. And every one of them was tied up fast and couldn't move an inch, just because they didn't know about the frogs. And then the sun came out, and we were way down the river with a clear channel, and all safe and sound. And the frogs that were ahead swam back to the shantyboat, and we all sang *My Country 'Tis Of Thee* together. And everybody was feeling fine.

The days went by without much trouble for a while. We'd ground on a sand bar now and then, and we had more fogs and more storms, and we couldn't ever get the roof fixed to keep out the rain. But all of us were keeping the pact. Even the snake and the rabbit were good friends now. Lucky thing for the rabbit, too, because one day he was looking at himself in the water, trying to do some tricks with his ears, and he got scared of something and fell overboard. He'd have drowned sure if it hadn't been for Judge Black whipping out and coiling around him, and pulling him onto the deck. The rabbit looked pretty scared for a minute, and I think he was more afraid of having a snake wrapped around him than he was of the water. But Judge Black handled him as if he was a robin's egg. And I looked at the Judge's eyes and they were clear as well water.

When he could get his breath, the rabbit thanked him and said how wonderful of him it was to do it.

"A friend in need is a friend indeed," the Judge answered.

He was a fine fellow, was Judge Black.

We were down below Natchez now, in the Cajun country. It was an early season, and there was fruit everywhere, and the biggest watermelons you ever saw were lying in the fields. But they were all fenced in, and people were standing behind the fences, watching with big dogs and guns. Our mouths watered when we saw those melons—there's nothing like a ripe watermelon when you're going down the river. But we knew we could never get one without being torn to pieces.

Then late in the afternoon we saw a field with melons so pretty we just couldn't pass without stopping a minute. So we anchored the shanty, and looked through the chicken-wire fence.

We were still standing there when a big bull that was grazing off a little way came up to us. He was a pretty rough looking fellow with his long horns and red eyes and I thought for a minute we were going to have trouble, but after he began talking I could see he was really good-natured.

"Those melons are as good as they look," he said. "And it's part of my job to watch out for this end of the planta-

tion. But the farmer I work for isn't a
hog. He knows and I know you can
break in and do a lot of damage. So I
always make a deal with fellows like
you. You pick out any melon you want,
the ripest one there is in the patch, and
have a good time. But don't touch any
others. If you take a single bite out of
a second one, I'll go up to the barn and
tell the dogs. If you look hard you'll
see the gate's open."

And he went away.

We saw the gate was unlocked the
way he said and we stood outside so
excited we couldn't talk hardly. And
before we went in we were trying to
figure out how to find the ripest—if you
know anything about melons you know
that's harder than trying to straighten a

kink in your tail—when the fox spoke up and asked us to let him do the picking. I thought there was a funny look in his eye. But you can't tell about foxes.

"You've heard about redheaded people being able to find water with a forked stick," he said. "A red fox can pick a ripe melon the same way. Only instead of a stick he uses his tail."

We all squeezed through the gate, and the melons were all around us, big as rain barrels. The fox went up to the biggest.

"Watch my tail close," he told us. "I'm going to walk over every melon here. If my tail hangs down, the melon's sour as vinegar. But if my tail stands straight up, the melon's ripe and sweet as honey."

He began marching up and down the patch with all of us following close behind. A couple of times we saw his tail quiver, and we thought we had what we were looking for. But in a second it dropped flat to the ground again.

We went over every melon, and his tail didn't straighten up once.

The fox shook his head. "That bull cheated us," he said. "They're all so green a single piece would give you colic."

We went back to the shanty disgusted. And then the sun set, and we saw the bull come up and look around, and then a farm boy locked the gate and took him off to the barn for the night. It got dark right after that and we went to sleep hungry.

Well, about the time the owls were calling second midnight, I waked up with a noise in the shanty. And I rolled over and saw the fox sneaking out the door. I remembered that funny look in his eye when he was testing the melons, and now I was sure he was up to something. I followed him along the bank, keeping in the shadows so he wouldn't know I was there. First thing he went over to the melon patch and dug under the chicken wire, till he struck rock and couldn't go any deeper. And then he squeezed himself through the hole. He was gone for a little while, and when he came back his face was all wet and sticky with something, and his jaws were dripping. He squeezed under the wire and came outside a minute, and then went back, sort of testing the fence and measuring the hole with his paws. He did this ten times, I guess. And each time his eyes were shining brighter and his jaws were dripping faster. At last I couldn't stand it any longer, so I crawled under, too. I saw him, with his head buried in a melon he had just about finished, so ripe even in the moonlight it was red as a poppy.

I called him, and he jumped so hard, if he'd have hit against anything he'd have burned his fur. I asked him what he was doing. And then he confessed, how he knew we could only have one melon, and how he was crazy about watermelons, and one watermelon for five animals wouldn't go anywhere. So he'd made up the story about his tail picking the ripe ones, and that way when he said none of them were good, he had the whole melon to himself. I asked him why he came in and out the hole so many times, and he said it was to see how much he could eat, and still not be too swelled up to get outside the fence again. He said foxes always measure themselves that way when it's a tight squeeze.

We walked back to the shanty, and I told him what a terrible thing it was he'd done to us. How he'd broken the pact, and betrayed his brothers. He knew without my saying, and hung his head, and didn't try to defend himself. Just said he was terribly sorry, and it was his lower nature coming out, and he'd take any punishment we decided.

I woke up the others, and we talked it over a long time. A pact's a pact, and you can't have it broken. And we couldn't expect to ever reach New Orleans and get what we wanted unless we all worked together and trusted each other to the end. At first we were going to put him off the shanty, but he begged so hard, we decided to let him stay and try to redeem himself. Only until that time, we said, we'd act as if he wasn't there. When he started doing any of the tricks he always liked to do, we'd look somewhere else; when he spoke to us, we wouldn't answer. It'd be as if he was a ghost fox, that we couldn't see or hear. And since he was such a terrible show-off, that was the worst punishment of all. Many a time after that he started talking, all smiling and friendly. And we all got up and walked away. And his eyes would get shiny and his body would shiver all over. It was really pitiful.

Well, more days passed, and it was getting time for us to be in New Orleans if we were going to be there when the

Catfish Bend farmers arrived, so we began to hurry. We got up earlier every morning and kept going every afternoon till long after dark. And all the time the water was getting higher and higher, and we'd see big islands of drift floating. And we knew poor Catfish was going to have plenty of trouble again. Pretty soon New Orleans began coming closer and closer. We went by Plaquemine where the big locks take you out to Texas, and St. Rose where Captain Dick lives that runs the *Tennessee Belle*, and then we saw the big highway bridge, and we were sure all our troubles were over, because New Orleans wasn't any distance away.

We tied up for a while, because the water was terribly fast here, and I wanted to find out about the channel. The bridge had big concrete piers out in the water, and if we weren't careful, they'd break the boat into matchsticks.

I was just starting to go ashore and ask the way of a couple of otters running around on the bank, when all of a sudden a big towboat went past, making tremendous waves. And in a minute the rope holding us to the land broke and we started racing down the river. We went faster and faster as the full current caught us, and a mole could have seen that we were heading straight for a bridge pier. We were still close to the shore, and there was a chance of saving ourselves if we could find a rope to throw over something. But there was only one rope on the shanty when we

found it, and now that was gone. It certainly looked like the finish. And then, just as we were passing a little cabin on the bank, I saw Judge Black twist the end of his tail around a cleat on the shanty and shoot out his long body toward a pine tree.

He looped around it, and the boat

stopped with a bump that nearly sent us all into the water. It was a wonderful thing of him to do. It must have almost pulled him in two.

He stretched three or four inches while I was watching, and I could see by his eyes how he was suffering. "You've got to get another rope," he panted. "I can't hold on but a few minutes. My whole backbone's coming apart."

And I heard a loud crack inside him.

He'd saved us and given us a new chance. But I knew it would be all wasted if we didn't do something fast. That bridge pier was still out there, with the racing water. And then I saw a rope on the porch of the cabin that was under the tree, and a dog sitting

near it, a big dog, sort of like a shep-
herd, ragged and old, and scratching
himself with both hind legs like he was
crazy. I called out to him and asked him
to throw me the rope.

He shook his head and scratched
harder. "It's not my rope," he answered.
"And I haven't got the strength to
throw anything. These fleas have got
me all worn out. They're worse than
chiggers and measles and St. Vitus'
dance put together."

I tried to make him change his mind.
But the old dog was so miserable with
the fleas, he didn't listen. Or maybe he
couldn't hear, he was scratching so hard.

There was another loud crack inside
Judge Black. "I'm breaking up," he said.

And I was sure that was the end.

Just then the fox, who hadn't spoken to anybody for days—he was feeling so bad about the watermelons—leaned way over the edge of the boat, and got as near to the old dog as he could.

"If I show you how to get rid of your fleas will you throw us the rope?" he called out.

The old dog heard that all right, and sat up fast. "I'm too old for miracles," he said.

But you could see by his ears he was interested.

"Throw it," called the fox.

The old dog waited a minute, not sure what to do, and then tossed it over. I made it fast to a stump on shore, and then Judge Black could let go.

We stretched him out on the deck,

and his eyes were closed, and we thought for a while he was dead. But we kept throwing water over him, and after a while his eyes opened, and he raised his head and hissed a little, that nice, pleasant hiss you didn't mind at all. And we massaged his back, and rubbed him down with some leaves like bay leaves he told us that snakes always use for rheumatism—they get backache all the time, with such a long backbone. And then he sort of cleared his throat and took one of his cough drops, and we knew he'd be all right. And then I went off with the fox to see that he kept his promise to the dog. I was worried, too, I can tell you, because I thought maybe this was just another of his tricks. And it's no fun to make a fool of any big animal, even if he is a little old.

The fox rubbed against the dog a minute so that a few of the fleas jumped on him, and then went off a little way where there was a kind of pool by a sand bar and the water was quiet.

"Watch close," he said, and took a big leaf in his mouth and then walked into the water. He kept going forward, deeper and deeper, but very slow, so that the fleas had time to climb up to

that part of his body that was still dry. And pretty soon only his head was showing, and all the fleas were collected there. And then he brought his head down lower and lower until only his nose was showing, and of course the fleas went there, too. And then he dipped his nose and there wasn't anything showing but the leaf. In no time all the fleas were out on that. And then he let the leaf go, and they all floated down the river.

The old dog couldn't wait to try it himself, and got so excited he let the leaf fall a couple of times before he did it right. And then when he found they were really gone, he was a changed animal. He ran up and down the bank, barking like a puppy, and then he raced off and told all the other dogs, and they did it, too, because the fleas were bad. The pool was full of dogs splashing everywhere. They were all as happy as the old dog afterwards, and they went off and brought us the best things that were in the houses around there to eat. We had a wonderful time. And of course we knew it was the fox that had done it, so we forgave him, and took him back in the pact.

IV

WELL, WE got to the edge of New Orleans next day. And we ran the boat up a little bayou where the brother of the farmer at Catfish Bend lived in a little cabin on the bank, and where I'd found out from the old horse he always stayed when he came to New Orleans. We tied up in some trees where people and dogs wouldn't notice us. The Catfish farmer hadn't arrived yet, but he came down next day driving the wagon, with a couple of his neighbors riding on the seat, and two or three other wagons with more people behind. The farmer told his brother how they were going in town to see the Engineers. And his brother climbed up beside him, and we decided we ought to go along, too. We hid in the back of the wagon under an old tarpaulin, and started down the road. On the way the farmer kept pointing out the big levees everywhere that kept the floods from bothering the city, and saying how wonderful it would be if they'd fix up Catfish Bend the same way.

Well, after a while we were right in the middle of New Orleans, and I tell you I was pretty scared, even if we were under the tarpaulin and couldn't see too much. Automobiles running in every direction, puffing and honking, and the drivers yelling at each other like wildcats. And everywhere you looked people were getting ready for the Mardi gras, that's the big Carnival they have every year, building fancy painted floats and things. And then we went on to the Engineers. A soldier was standing there with a gun, and the farmer went up to him and told how they'd come down from Catfish Bend and what they wanted.

The soldier answered him just the way the old horse said he would, telling him they were all too busy. The farmer said could he talk to the old General that I could see walking around inside, with big teeth and mustaches looked just like a muskrat.

And the soldier said he was up in Baton Rouge, and wouldn't be back till Sunday.

The farmer and the others decided to
see the Mayor, and drove off to a big
building and went inside. I ran around
the walls, keeping in the bushes as much
as I could, till I heard the farmer's voice,
and then I climbed a tree that was there,
and looked in the window.

It was a big room with a lot of people
going in and out, and the Mayor was
there talking to the farmers, a sleepy-
eyed, bald-headed man with a big fat
stomach that made him sit way back

from his desk. He was always making faces, as if something was hurting him inside, and then he'd put a kind of powder in a glass and it all fizzed up and he'd drink it, the way I've seen the animal doctor at Catfish fix something for the cows when they had stomach trouble.

"Can't do anything for you, friends," he told the farmers, talking slow and important. "Too busy. I've got policemen and firemen and street cleaners to look after, and a new election in November. And I've got the new Mardi gras to get ready in a few weeks, and that's the biggest job of all. Besides I've got terrible indigestion. Have a cigar on your way out, friends."

The farmer began arguing with him.

And pretty soon the Mayor got mad, and his face turned all red, and a big policeman came up and grabbed the farmer and pushed him out the door. And the farmer's face got white, and he and the others went back to the wagon. And I climbed down from the tree and went back, too.

We drove up the street toward the bayou, and saw all the people getting ready for the Carnival again, building grandstands for the big parades and

making fancy costumes, and practicing fancy dancing. And in one place we saw a man and woman that the horse said were going to be King and Queen of the Carnival, and they were sitting around on thrones with big gold crowns on their heads, telling the other people what to do. Wherever we went everybody was laughing and singing.

But the farmer didn't laugh. He didn't speak for an hour maybe, just sat there looking like he was made of stone. Then he turned to his brother. "I'd like to show 'em," he said. "If I could, I'd stop their Mardi gras."

It was a long way to the bayou and we were getting terribly hungry. Once the farmer stopped to buy something in a grocery store, and we hopped out, too. They had wonderful things to eat in the store windows, but it wasn't like out in the fields around Catfish where you could just help yourself to whatever you wanted. You couldn't get a bite. Then a man dropped a bag when he was getting into an automobile. And we ran up and opened it, and there were some little boxes with fine things inside, corn, and green beans, and beautiful strawberries. And we started to eat. And I jerked back, like I was eating fire. They were all frozen, just like ice, and we had to leave them in the street. A big rat was hiding in a sewer grating by a butcher shop next door, and he told us that New Orleans people froze things that way on purpose.

The farmers and the others were still hardly talking when they got back to his brother's house. It was dark by then and they just sat around on the porch, without even lighting a lamp, and when people do that, you know things are bad. And every once in a while the farmer would say how they'd all just wasted their time, and they might as well never have come.

We went over to the shanty, and sat around feeling worse than the people.

"Nothing to do but go back home, I guess," Judge Black told us. And when Judge Black said something, you generally knew it was so.

The fox nodded. "An animal'd starve to death around here. The garbage cans are shut so tight they look like they've got locks on 'em. And a couple of places I saw people *burning* garbage."

Even the rabbit was serious. "Never saw such terrible people. They freeze their food and burn their garbage."

They all began talking about what they'd do when they got back up the Valley. But I remembered how I saw the drift coming down when we were driving along the top of the levee, with the river getting higher and higher. And I thought about all the days we'd spent on the mound, and all the bad times the other animals around Catfish would be having right now, and I begged them to stay a little longer.

I sat by the window and watched the lights of the city coming on in the distance. It was pretty. But I'd rather have

the stars. And then I began studying about things. The others lay down to get some sleep, and I was still studying. That's the way it is with a raccoon. You get him started studying, and he won't stop till he's got things all studied out.

It got later and later, and there wasn't a sound on the shanty, except the fox beating his tail against the floor the way he did in his sleep sometimes, I guess when he was dreaming about rabbits. And just then a little excursion boat landed at a dock near us, and some people came down the gangplank, all dressed in fancy costumes from a party they were having getting ready for the

Mardi gras. And a band came after them, all dressed in blue uniforms with blue feathers in their hats. And I remembered how all my life I heard from the animals down river how Mardi gras is the biggest thing in New Orleans. I guess maybe from the way people talk and come to see it from all over, it's the biggest thing anywhere in the world. And I got to thinking what the farmer said he'd like to do.

And then I had my idea. And I woke the others and told them about it. We went up the bayou a little way where it was open country and we could be out in the moonlight and feel a little more like we were at Catfish. We sat all night under a big live oak tree, talking and making our plans. If the New

Orleans people wouldn't help get the levees fixed at Catfish, we would stop their Mardi gras.

I went over to tell the old horse that belonged to the farmer.

"Won't work," he grumbled, the way he always did. "That's what's wrong with you woods animals. Always getting excited about some new idea. Trouble with you fellows is you don't eat oats. There's something that'll keep you calm. If everybody ate oats it'd be a better world."

Well, you know how there are plenty of big swamps right back of New Orleans, and as soon as I could I took the fox and went up the bayou. The fox talked to all the other foxes we met, and told them about our troubles and about the pact, and asked them to help us. And I did the same thing with all the raccoons. There wasn't a single animal that said no. They were still living too close to the river not to know about floods. They hadn't forgotten like everybody in New Orleans. An animal remembers things ten times longer than people. He lives a shorter time, but he remembers harder. We asked them to spread the word as much as they could.

We hurried back to the shanty, and as soon as it was dark we saw they'd kept their promise. Everywhere raccoons and foxes began coming out of the swamps, hundreds and thousands of them, all bound for New Orleans. And we went along. I didn't like it very much going down those narrow streets.

But when we got there you never saw
such carrying on. We raced through
alleys, and ran across gardens, and
hopped over back fences, always making as much noise as we could. We knew
the New Orleans dogs were all city dogs
had never smelled a wild animal before,
and we knew what we were doing

would drive them crazy. The dogs chased everywhere after us, barking and howling till we left just before daylight. And of course with such a terrible

racket nobody could sleep a wink.

We went into town again the next night, and every night after that, too. And in a few days everybody in New

Orleans was going around half asleep, and so tired and jumpy they were barking at each other almost like the dogs. And then the fox found out where the Mayor lived with one of those brown, nasty little dogs had a face all wrinkled like a potato and a squawk like a chicken. And we kept running up to the window and looking in, and the little dog kept yelling all night. And we did the same thing with the man and woman that were going to be King and Queen of the Mardi gras, and the other big people of the Carnival. So they had it the worst of all.

Well, after a week everybody in New Orleans was so worn out work on the Mardi gras almost stopped. And there were big stories in the papers about the wild animals coming into town, and wondering what made them act that way.

The farmer from Catfish went to talk to the Mayor again. We didn't go because he didn't have a tarpaulin in the wagon this time, and I couldn't take a chance on the New Orleans dogs in the daytime. But the old horse told me about it.

"My farmer's no fool," he said, not quite as grumpy as usual. "He knows there's something funny going on. He told the Mayor he figured the animals were coming into New Orleans because they were driven out of the swamps by high water, and if the animals felt that way maybe the Mayor could see it was worse with the people, and wouldn't he help 'em get the levees. And the Mayor said no, the way he did before."

We decided the Mayor and the rest of them in New Orleans needed another lesson.

"Do or die," said Judge Black, and he told us this time it was his turn to try. I went out to the swamps with him, and he talked to the snakes. He didn't have to say very much. You just looked at Judge Black, and you did what he said.

Next day when the New Orleans people woke up every place they went was full of snakes—green snakes and red snakes and black snakes and yellow snakes, snakes crawling up the kitchen sinks and sometimes in the beds. And plenty of 'em weren't nice snakes like

Judge Black. They were moccasins and rattlers that had terrible tempers, and would kill you if they got mad.

But the snakes didn't help any more than the raccoons and the foxes. There wasn't anything to do but try a third time. I noticed the frog's stomach swelling up like a watermelon again, and I knew he'd thought of something.

"Leave it to me," he croaked, and I went with him up the bayou. He'd stop whenever he saw some swamp frogs sitting together, and they asked him a lot of questions about the Indian Bayou Glee Club, what kind of music they were singing around Catfish now, and whether he'd learned any new pieces. And after a while we came home feeling mighty good. Anybody who's been out in the country knows how many mosquitoes there are in a swamp, and I guess everybody knows how many mosquitoes a single frog can swallow. The frogs had promised not to eat a single mosquito till we gave them the word.

Well, a few days afterward we were sitting out on the shanty, when the rabbit turned the color of a ghost.

"Fire!" he yelled, and jumped into the bayou.

I swung around and saw what looked like thick black smoke rolling out of the swamps. But when I looked harder I saw it wasn't smoke at all. It was clouds of the most terrible mosquitoes that ever flew, heading straight toward the middle of New Orleans.

Well, Judge Black jumped in and got

the rabbit out in a hurry the way he did before, and gave him a long talking to about being so silly, and we all sat back and watched those mosquitoes go past, with a hum so loud it sounded like a train whistle. We had to duck inside, and if you put a paw a quarter of an inch out of the window, in a few seconds a thousand mosquitoes would be chewing it to pieces. You can guess what it was like in town.

It wasn't only Louisiana mosquitoes. News travels fast in the swamps, and when they heard how the frogs had stopped eating, mosquitoes came from all over. The New Orleans people tried everything. But the mosquitoes kept getting thicker and thicker. Nobody could go out in the street unless they wore hats with mosquito bars over their faces. The Mardi gras people tried practicing their dances all covered with mosquito bars. And plenty of times the band would start playing. But the minute anybody moved the mosquitoes were under the netting like smoke; the people made so much noise slapping their arms and legs you could hardly have heard it thunder. Of course nobody could do anything about getting ready for Mardi gras.

The frog was terribly proud, and he swelled up so much we were afraid he would burst. His stomach kept getting bigger and bigger, until pretty soon it was all out of control, and all he could do was watch it grow.

But Judge Black and I made some cold packs with icy water from a spring near the bayou, and we got his stomach down again.

But the mosquitoes didn't work either. We tried a couple of other things, but it was the same way. And more farmers came down from Catfish in their wagons because the floods were getting so bad there, and went to see the Mayor. New Orleans was getting mighty worried now. And I heard from the horse how the King and Queen and the other big Carnival people told the Mayor how all the visitors that had come were leaving, and how terrible it would be if there wasn't a Mardi gras that year. And people from all over were sending word to the Mayor, saying how it would be like the sun not rising, and how maybe people would even forget how to dance and sing for the rest of their lives if New Orleans didn't have the Carnival. And plenty in New Orleans said they couldn't understand all the queer things that were happening and maybe it was a punishment or something; they thought maybe if the Mayor would help the Catfish people, it might change their luck, and the Mardi gras could begin.

The Mayor was all worn out with no sleep and mosquito bites and everybody complaining. But he wouldn't change his mind.

eeeeeeeeeeeeeeeeeeeeeeeeeeeeeeeeeeeeeeeeeeeee

V

WELL, THINGS were looking pretty bad.
I heard from the horse how the farmer
was ready to quit, and was saying how
even if it was flooded up at Catfish, it
was better than being with people like
the Mayor. I wasn't feeling too good
myself. I was still sore all over from a
terrible night a bloodhound gave me,
chasing me through the streets for three
or four hours, and he would have had
me if I hadn't climbed a big pole all
covered with wires that had sparks
coming out—But I'd rather not even
think about it, much less talk.

We were sitting on the shanty after

dark, looking out over the river, when we heard a clump, clump on the bank of the bayou. It was the horse, and I was surprised, because he'd never been to see us before.

"Came over to tell you," he grumbled. "The farmer's leaving before daybreak. I thought you ought to know."

And he turned and started back up the bayou.

Well, I knew that was the finish. Here we'd worked day and night for weeks, and now it was all going to end in nothing.

I ran after him down the road.

"You can't let the farmer go," I said.

He stopped dead in his tracks. "What's your meaning?" he asked.

"I mean you've got to keep him

here," I said. "You've got to give us time to think."

The horse looked at me as if I was crazy. "How can I stop him?" he grumbled. "It's a man's world. Not a horse's."

"It is only if you think it is," I told him. "What'd happen if you went lame?"

"Oh that," he mumbled. Then he shook his head. "Don't like it. Plenty of horses do it, but I won't. Never played that kind of trick on him before. Don't want to start playing tricks on him now."

Honestly, sometimes that horse didn't have more sense than the rabbit. I explained to him how it wasn't a trick, that it was for the horses and animals everywhere, and reminded him of those horses up at Dismal, some of them friends of his, that were almost drowned in the flood last year.

I guess the reminding did it.

"All right," he said. "Won't do any good, but I'll keep him till twelve noon tomorrow. Not a minute later. I don't want to be on the road all night. There's a big wildcat up around Canebrake, and I don't want him jumping on my back in the dark."

I came back to the shanty.

"It's the end of the world," said the frog.

And they all began to pack again to go back home.

I went to the river and walked up and down the bank. And I thought,

harder than I ever thought before. Every now and then I'd see some animal going down on a bunch of driftwood, and once a tree bumped against the shore, and there was an old squirrel on it came from Preacher Bend, that's almost nine miles below Catfish. And he said the flood was terrible, and the wild animals were all having the worst time he'd ever seen. And I decided I couldn't give up.

Well, it got later and later, and it was just before dawn, with that queer feeling comes over you when the night's changing into day, and there were only a few more hours left. And then I saw a couple of muskrats sitting in their holes on the riverbank. And I knew what I had to do.

I rushed back up the bayou to talk to the old horse. On the way I saw Judge Black coiled up in front of the shanty, taking the early morning air, and I told him my plan. But I didn't tell the others, because I knew there'd be terrible trouble if anybody found out, and the rabbit was an awful gossip. I found the horse acting lame like he'd promised, and he said he'd do what I asked.

I spoke to some young muskrats and they told me to go see a muskrat lived in a tunnel along the riverbank. I found him after a while, an old fellow with whiskers looked like the General I saw in the Engineer office at New Orleans, and I talked to him all morning. A muskrat's pretty hard to talk to, harder than most animals. Some say they're sort of thick-headed from digging holes in the ground all the time, and maybe a little slow. But I've always gotten along with them pretty well. I told this old muskrat what I wanted. But he wouldn't say yes for sure.

"I'll do the best I can," he told me. "But muskrats today aren't what they used to be. All these young muskrats want is a good time."

So I couldn't figure out what was going to happen. Going back I saw that the river was still getting higher, way above the level of the town now, with only the big levee keeping out the water. When you looked up you could see the big steamboats going past over your head, like it always is when there's high water in New Orleans. If you don't know about levees, it gives you a funny feeling.

Well, noon came, and I went over with the other animals to where the farmer was hitching the horse in the wagon, because he wasn't playing lame now, and we crawled under the tarpaulin the way we did before. Pretty soon the farmer climbed onto the seat, and the other people jumped in their wagons, too, and got in line behind. And the farmer flicked the reins, and they started on the road back home.

But the old horse hadn't gone more than a few feet, when he suddenly turned the wagon clear around and started down the road to New Orleans. The farmer tried to steer him back again up the river, but the horse wouldn't go.

The farmer was worried. "Never saw him do anything like this in his life before," he said to the others.

He tried and tried half an hour maybe; for a minute it would look as if the horse was going all right, and then he'd swing around again and head straight for town.

The farmer shook his head. "That's a smart horse," he muttered. "He's got some kind of reason. Maybe it's a sign we ought to go and see the Mayor just once more."

They talked it over and decided they would. He was a stubborn farmer, and hated to give up anyway.

Well, we got down to the building where the Mayor was, and the farmers all went inside, and we climbed up on the window sill.

The Mayor was sitting at his desk with his fat head so swollen up from mosquito bites he could hardly see, and he could sit a foot closer to his desk, he was that much thinner. He was making faces like his stomach hurt him all the time now, and drinking his glasses of fizzy water one right after another. He looked so bad I almost felt sorry for him.

The Mayor's office was crowded

with people, and the man and woman who were going to be King and Queen of the Carnival were there, and the others helping with the Mardi gras, some of them in their fancy costumes. And they were all arguing and making angry speeches. And then the people from Catfish came in, and the farmer began talking the way he always did about the floods. And everybody started arguing louder, and the Mayor banged on the desk with his fist and said no again, and the farmer and the others started to leave.

And just then a man came running through the door, his face as white as mine the time I found a bag of flour. "The levee's breaking at the end of the street!" he shouted. "The water's coming through in a hundred places!"

And right behind him another man came yelling. "The levees are breaking all over! Everybody run for their lives!"

Well, the place went crazy. Some of the people ran to the doors, and some just stood where they were, quiet as if they were praying. And the Mayor began calling for police and firemen, and shouting for people to get out on the levees, and all over bells began to ring and whistles to blow, loud enough to make you deaf. Only the farmer and the other Catfish people didn't get excited. They were used to floods. The farmer raced down the street in his wagon, and we went with him, and the other farmers came behind. And they

began piling up sandbags and earth, trying to plug up the places where the water was pouring through. And some of the New Orleans people came along and did the same way.

For a little while it didn't seem to do any good, and the water began filling up the streets by the levee and rushing into the cellars. And the bells rang louder, and the firewagons and police cars and ambulances went around screaming like wildcats, and people ran up and down every which way, like an anthill when you happen to kick it with your paw.

But the farmers just kept piling the sandbags higher. And pretty soon the water slowed up and stopped, and the streets began to dry again. Then the New Orleans people gave a big cheer and started going home.

The Catfish people were getting ready to leave, too, when the big policeman that always stood by the Mayor's door came up to the farmer and said the Mayor wanted to see him. And he went back to the office, and the Mayor looked ashamed, and said they all wanted to thank him and the others for helping save New Orleans. The Mayor said he was sorry for acting the way he did. They'd forgotten what it was like to worry about floods in New Orleans, he said, and now they'd learned their lesson, and they were going to help get things fixed up at Catfish. And the old General of the Engineers that looked like a muskrat was there, and he said he'd start his men working as soon as he could.

New Orleans people are really nice. They just had to be reminded, like the horse. I guess most people are that way, a little slow in the head, like the muskrats. You can't expect everybody to be smart as a raccoon.

We started back to the wagon, and then all of a sudden I missed Judge Black, and for a few minutes we were afraid he'd been killed by an automobile. And then we saw him coming out of a sewer. He'd seen a drain pipe coming down from the Mayor's window, and being so excited about everything and being a snake, he forgot what he was doing and crawled into it, and then he couldn't crawl back.

So everything was fine. They asked the farmers to stay for Mardi gras, and we stayed, too. And they had the best Mardi gras ever was in New Orleans, with people dressed like clowns and wild men and monkeys, and beautiful parades of floats all covered with gold and silver, and lights at night that were brighter than the moon. And in the big parade at the end they had a special float for the farmers, and shot off fireworks, and took their pictures, and wrote stories about the wonderful thing they'd done for New Orleans. And we watched the farmers ride by and laughed our heads off, because we knew what had really happened. The farmers hadn't helped to save the town. There hadn't been a flood at all. The muskrats had just bored some little holes in the levee, the way I asked, and then after a while when I gave the sign, plugged them up again.

Well, we turned the shanty over to some wharf rats that said they'd like to have it, and took the wagon back to

Catfish, because it's hard getting a shantyboat up stream. And pretty soon the Government Engineers came and started work, and there was a parade at Catfish, this time just for the farmer, and we nearly died laughing again.

That's the way it is with people. They think they do everything. But we

didn't mind really. They were all having a fine time, and they left the lids off their garbage cans every night.

Well, now you know the way we got the levees here at Catfish. And we haven't had a flood in a coon's age.

It shows what you can do when you have a pact.

ΩΩΩΩΩΩΩΩΩΩΩΩΩΩΩΩΩΩΩΩΩΩΩΩΩΩΩΩΩΩΩΩΩΩ

The raccoon stopped talking, and I was going to ask him some questions, when the whistle of the *Tennessee Belle* blew, and I had to hurry off. The last I saw of him he was washing his paw, because I had shaken hands with him again.

I walked onto the boat where the mate was watching the crew of the

Government dredge working on the levee.

"These farmers at Catfish did a wonderful job the way they got the Engineers up here," the mate remarked.

I didn't answer anything.

It's like my friend said. You can't expect everybody to be smart as a raccoon.

Ben Lucien Burman

THE OWL HOOTS TWICE
AT CATFISH BEND

Here is a madcap tale about a wolf in fox's clothing and the havoc he causes when the peaceful animals of Catfish Bend rescue him from his pursuers—and then listen to his evil advice! Like *High Water at Catfish Bend*, which critics ranked with the best of "Uncle Remus," *The Owl Hoots Twice at Catfish Bend* is at once a genial satire on the absurdities of our time, an exciting adventure story, and a rich entertainment that will keep readers young and old chuckling over every page.

Ben Lucien Burman

BLOW A WILD BUGLE FOR CATFISH BEND

Here is a rollicking adventure story about the animals at Catfish Bend, as, led by their mayor Doc Raccoon, Judge Black the snake, and clever J.C. the fox, they travel to Tickpaw marsh to help fight off a terrible invasion—coyotes with a master plan to finish off all the animals along the Mississippi. Readers familiar with the universal appeal of the series will welcome this genial satire in the best *Catfish Bend* tradition.

Ben Lucien Burman

SEVEN STARS FOR CATFISH BEND

When the animals at Catfish Bend learned that the State planned to give their peaceful swamp away to hunters, they knew they had to find a way to save their home. How the animals decide to stay and fight for Catfish Bend makes a thrilling story—and, true to the *Catfish Bend* tradition, a rich entertainment and genial satire that will amuse readers of all ages.